Not so long ago, in a city you most likely have heard of and may even have been to, a soon to be middle-aged, balding dad was lying in bed, reading good night stories to his little baby daughter.

While lying there with the little one in his arms, he noticed something strange. It seemed that all princesses in these fairy tales needed to be saved and that their most important characteristic was their beauty.

He did not like that at all. He didn't want his daughter to grow up in this kind of world. So, while reading, he started changing little words here and there. All of a sudden, a 'beautiful' princess became a 'brave' one, and he saw the sparkle in his daughter's eyes!

From this came the idea of **Fairy Tales Retold**, with a simple, yet powerful premise:

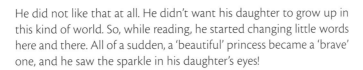

Changing one word can change everything!

Encouraged by the response to our idea, we are starting to dream about the impact this project can have on children around the world, and we can't help but get excited!

So, if you enjoy our retelling, please spread the word about the new Snow White so that this story too will have its own fairy tale ending.

Lena & Luka,
this is your book.

Danke!

SNOW WHITE
and the Seven Dwarfs

EASTERN
Blue Bird

LOVE
to read

bruise
&
SCRATCH

Stephan Kalinski & Iain Botterill

Claudia Piras

FAIRY
TALES
Re-
told

Once upon a time, long, long ago, an adventurous King and wise Queen ruled over a distant land. The Queen was kind and wise, and the King adventurous and just. They were adored and respected by all in their realm and seemed as happy as any couple could possibly be.

There was, however, one sad part of the King's and Queen's life. They longed for a child but didn't have one.

One early spring morning, the Queen was sewing whilst gazing out of her ebony window at the beautiful, blue sky. Suddenly a bird flew by, startling the Queen and she pricked her finger with a needle.

A single drop of blood fell onto the windowsill. Staring at it glistening in the sun, she said:

"Oh, how I wish we had a child with eyes as blue as the sky, lips as red as blood, and hair as black as ebony."

4

A few weeks later, the Queen touched her stomach and smiled. She could feel she was pregnant and ran to the King to tell him the great news.

Their dream had become true!

Soon after, during a glorious winter storm which covered the castle and its garden in a magical blanket of snow, the Queen gave birth to a baby girl with eyes as blue as the sky, lips as red as blood, and hair as black as ebony.

The next morning, the storm had passed. The new parents, holding the little baby girl in their arms, gazed out the window as the sun's rays danced on the freshly fallen, powdery snow. It was then that they knew and whispered to each other:

"Welcome to the world, Snow White!"

The King and Queen were happier than ever before.

But when Snow White was only a few months old, the Queen caught a mysterious illness and died. The King, and everyone in the realm was devastated.

Three years passed with the King taking care of his little Snow White.

Although it was hard being a single parent, he managed quite well and taught the little Princess how to read, write, and draw.

Then, one day, the King fell in love again and remarried. The new Queen was incredibly brave and even kind. Having travelled alone from a distant land, she had conquered her fears to start a new life in the kingdom.

But her thirst for power had planted a seed of jealousy and wickedness in her heart. She started to study dark magic and bought a mirror that gave her powers over the King and all the land.

Every week she would ask:

"Mirror, mirror on the wall, who's the bravest of them all?"

And every week the mirror would answer:

"You, my Queen, you are the bravest of all."

This pleased the Queen greatly; she admired bravery more than anything else and knew that her magic mirror could never lie.

The Queen, who at first was very fond of the little Princess, saw over the years how brave Snow White was becoming.

She noticed it in small things, such as the time the little Princess overcame her fear of heights and climbed the tallest tree in the garden. Or when she conquered her anxiety and gave a welcome speech in front of hundreds of guests at the royal ball.

But, instead of being proud of her, the Queen could feel the jealousy in her heart growing and growing.

Then one morning, Snow White had just celebrated her seventh birthday, the Queen asked:

"Mirror, mirror on the wall, who's the bravest of them all?"

This time, however, the mirror replied:

"You, my Queen, are brave; it is true. But little Snow White is a thousand times braver than you."

The Queen, stunned by this answer, blankly stared at her magic mirror for what felt like an eternity.

No longer able to control herself, she flew into a jealous rage. Her anger was unlike anything her servants had ever seen as she screamed across the room for the court's Hunter.

When he appeared, she ordered him to grab Snow White and take her to the farthest corner of the magic forest.

"Once you're there," she thundered in a terrifying voice, *"take out your bow and arrow and kill her! Kill her and bring me back her heart!"*

The Hunter turned pale and stammered:

"I, I, I will do as you command my Queen."

He went at once and found the little Princess playing in the castle garden next to the tall tree. He told her that they would go on a small adventure together into the magic forest. Snow White, who loved adventures, became very excited and jumped up, ready to go.

As they walked through the forest, Snow White noticed the Hunter was behaving very strangely. They did not sing their favourite song together; in fact, he was barely speaking to her at all and seemed very nervous.

After walking for over an hour in near silence, they reached a corner of the forest that the Princess had never seen before.

Then, suddenly, the Hunter grabbed her hands, twisted them sharply and tied her up against a tree!

"What are you doing? Why are you tying me up?!" Snow White cried while trying to break free.

She saw a tear forming in the corner of the Hunter's eyes. *"I'm, I'm so sorry my little princess,"* he mumbled, slowly turning and walking away with the bow and arrow in his hands.

Snow White knew she had to act fast. She wrestled against the rope and called out:

"Wait, wait ... please!

Before you do what you must, grant me one last wish. Sing me the song that we always sang when we played together in the forest."

The Hunter was unable to look at her. Wiping away his tears, he began to sing their song for the very last time.

As he finished the final note, he turned around to shoot and kill the little Princess.

She was gone? She was gone!

A pile of rope lay at the foot of the tree. While he'd been singing, she must have wriggled free and escaped!

Looking down at the rope, a small smile escaped his lips; Snow White really was the bravest girl he'd ever known.

His happiness quickly turned to dread when he looked back towards the castle. He could never reveal the truth to the Queen.

He would have to lie!

Taking his bow and arrow, he found and shot a wild boar and took its heart to the Queen. She took the heart, looked at it with emptiness in her eyes, before simply dropping it into the cold white snow.

The little Princess, meanwhile, all alone in the great magic forest, was running and running and running. The trees seemed to whisper to each other, scaring even the brave Snow White, who carried on running as fast as she could. She ran over sharp stones and through thorns, as far as her feet could carry her.

Just as evening was about to fall, the Princess saw a small house down in the valley. She ran to it, knocked on the dark wooden door, and waited.

Nothing.

As the wind howled and rain began to fall, she took a deep breath and stepped inside.

Inside, everything was small but tidy. On the wall was a big map of the world with seven small flags pinned on it.

Next to the door were seven little pairs of slippers, neatly organized. In the dining room stood a little table with a tablecloth and seven colorful little plates and cups filled with food and drink.

Because she was so hungry, Snow White ate a few vegetables and a little bread from each plate; from each cup, she drank some milk.

Grabbing a piece of paper and a pencil, the Princess carefully drew a small heart and wrote:

"To Whomever lives here, please don't be upset or scared. I was in need of help and found your shelter. Thank You!"

She placed it on the table, walked upstairs, found the bedroom and immediately fell fast asleep.

After dark, the owners of the house returned. They were seven dwarfs who mined for gold in the mountains. Their names were Akashi, Shakti, Thiago, Leila, Egbo, Li and Sabrina. They had come from the seven corners of the earth, having travelled across land and sea in search of treasure.

The moment they opened the door, they knew someone had been there!

Akashi wondered:

"Who has been sitting in my chair?"

Shakti inquired:

"Who has been taking from my plate?"

Li asked:

"Who has been eating my bread?"

Leila said:

"Who has been stealing my vegetables?"

Egbo whispered:

"Who has been using my fork?"

Sabrina demanded:

"Who has been drinking from my cup"

Thiago decided to check the rest of the house.

When he peered into the bedroom, he found Snow White lying on his bed fast asleep.
He quietly called the others, who came running up and were amazed at what they saw:

"Oh, good heavens!" they whispered.

*"This child must have travelled through the magic forest all by herself! She must be so brave!
How did she do it?"*

27

The next morning Snow White woke up. She was confused.

"What is your name?" Sabrina asked,

"Snow White," she answered.

"How did you find your way to our house?" Shakti wanted to know.

It all came bursting out.

Snow White told them all about the Queen and her magic mirror, all about her escape from the Hunter and all about her terrifying journey through the magic forest to their house.

The dwarfs, amazed by her story, huddled together and whispered excitedly. Then, Akashi popped up and asked: *"Can you read?"*

"Why, yes I can." Snow White answered.

Then Egbo turned back, *"Can you write?"* She looked at him and nodded.

Finally, Leila spun around in amazement: *"And you can draw as well?!"* Snow White smiled and pointed to the piece of paper from last night.

After talking for a while, all seven turned around and said in unison:

"If you can protect the house while we work and teach us how to write, read and draw like you, then we would love you to stay with us. You will have everything that you could ever want."

Snow White, whose worry had grown while the dwarfs spoke amongst themselves, looked at the seven with a wide smile, clapped her hands with excitement and said:

"Yes, of course. I would love to protect the house for you and teach you all that I know!"

The Princess was not only brave but also very clever. She loved to read, write and draw. She was so excited about staying at the dwarfs' house and couldn't wait to learn more about each of them and the seven corners of the world they had come from.

Snow White lived happily alongside the dwarfs. Every morning the seven went off into the mountains looking for treasure, leaving the Princess at home with the animals from the magic forest, who kept her company.

In the evening, they came home and found the Princess had repaired little things here and there and had prepared lessons for each of them.

Back at the castle, the Queen was delighted. Knowing that she was the bravest woman in all the land, she had not spoken to the mirror since the Hunter had returned with Snow White's heart. But then one day, while walking past it, she asked:

"Mirror, mirror on the wall, who's the bravest of them all?"

"You, my Queen, are brave; it is true. But Snow White, living beyond the mountains with the seven dwarfs, is still a thousand times braver than you," it answered.

This stunned the Queen. She knew that the mirror never lied. The colour drained from her face as she realised, she had been deceived by the Hunter.

Snow White was still alive!

The Queen felt her jealousy bubbling up inside, as she almost exploded with anger. She took a deep breath and began to think and think.

"As long as Snow White is alive, I will never be the bravest woman in the land! There must be a way to get rid of her once and for all. No one else can be trusted." she muttered.

"This time, I will find a way to kill her myself!"

The Queen kept thinking and thinking until, at last, she came up with a cunning plan. She went up to her most secret room, which nobody else was allowed to enter, and carefully made a poisoned apple. It was beautiful; anyone who saw it would not be able to resist it.

But whoever ate, even the tiniest piece, would instantly die.

Covering her face, the Queen disguised herself as an old, gentle widow. She stepped out of the castle and began the long journey to the dwarfs' house.

When she arrived, she hid in the nearby bushes, waiting for the seven to set off and then knocked on the door.

Snow White opened the window.

"Hello old woman, who are you and how can I help?"

The Queen answered: "Hello, my dear, I'm just passing by and was wondering if I could come inside your house to rest."

"I'm sorry!" said the Princess, "I can't let anyone in who I don't know. The seven dwarfs have taught me that strangers can be dangerous for as long as the evil Queen is ruling the land."

"Don't you worry, that's quite all right, my dear," answered the old woman.

"If you don't mind, I will just sit and rest on your little bench."

Snow White nodded and smiled. She was happy to have someone to talk to, and the old lady seemed kind.

"My dear, would you like one of my delicious apples? I picked them myself this morning. Here, take one," said the Queen.

"Thank You so much, but I must say no," Snow White replied, *"I cannot accept anything from strangers, even ones as kind as you."*

"Are you afraid of poison?" asked the old lady with a smile. *"Don't Be. Here, I'll cut the apple in two, and we can share."*

The Princess had been working hard all morning and had forgotten to eat breakfast. The apple looked so delicious, and when the old woman eat her half, she simply could not resist.

She stuck out her hand and took the other half.

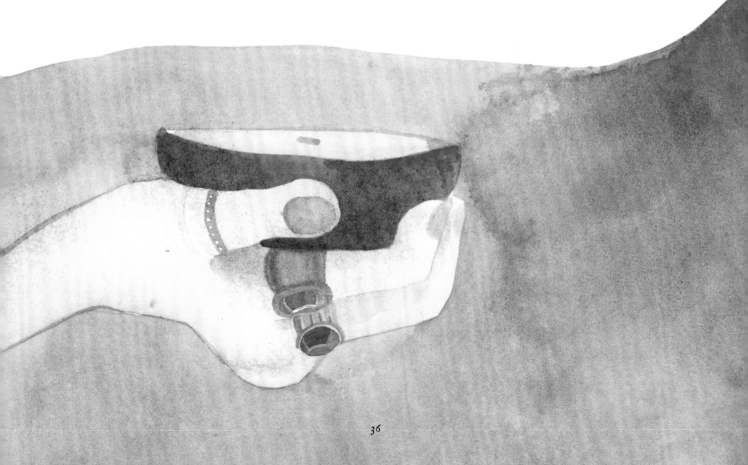

Snow White took one bite of the apple and collapsed onto the ground.

The Queen had made the apple so carefully that only the half she gave the Princess was poisoned. It worked instantly.

Snow White was dead!

The Queen took off her disguise and looked down at the Princess with an evil smile and said:

"Goodbye, Snow White. Your friends will never be able to save you now."

She quickly returned to the castle and, making sure she was alone, asked:

"Mirror, mirror on the wall, who's the bravest of them all?"

The mirror quickly and solemnly answered:

"You, my Queen, you are the bravest of all."

She smiled. At last, her cruel and jealous heart was at rest, as much as a cruel and jealous heart can ever be at rest!

When the dwarfs came home that evening, they found Snow White lying on the ground next to the window. As they came closer, they saw she was not moving or breathing at all. She seemed dead!

The dwarfs shouted and shook her, trying desperately to wake the Princess.

But nothing seemed to help!

They checked everywhere for injuries but found nothing. Eventually, they fell silent and stared despairingly at dear Snow White, knowing the worst was true.

The dwarfs carefully laid her on a bed of straw and sat next to her and mourned over her for seven days.

They then decided to build a beautiful grave, but since she still looked as fresh as a living person, Li said: *"It feels wrong to bury her in the black earth."*

The others noddingly agreed and spent the next week crafting a majestic glass coffin with Snow White's name engraved in gold letters on its' side.

They laid the Princess inside the coffin and carried her to the mountain top where Snow White had first seen their house many months ago. The dwarfs decided that one of them would always stay and watch over her, together with the animals of the forest.

More than ten years
passed, until one day, an
adventurous Prince entered the forest,
came across the dwarfs' house seeking shelter for
the night. He had seen Snow White's coffin on top of
the mountain.

Fascinated by the Princess, he said:

"Tell me more about the girl! Did you know her? What was she like? Why did she die? Why is she lying in a glass coffin?"

The dwarfs, with heavy hearts, explained:

"Snow White was the bravest girl we have ever known. She had a heart of gold. She taught us how to conquer our fears, and how to read, write and draw.

But one day, when we came back from the mountain, we found her lying dead on the ground."

"The poor Princess, she was so full of life, and we miss her so much! She never got the chance to fulfil her biggest dream: to discover the seven corners of the world.

We think the evil Queen killed her because she was jealous of her bravery."

While hearing the dwarfs tell their story the young, Prince became very sad.

A small tear rolled down his cheek, and his heart filled with anger and rage.

"I will find and kill this evil Queen for what she did to Snow White and for all the suffering she has caused!" he shouted.

The Prince leapt from his seat, ignoring the dwarfs' warnings of the evil Queen's magic powers, and jumped on his horse.

47

He rode up the mountain to have one last look at Snow White. Reaching the top, the Prince got off his horse. As he got closer, he stumbled over a root and fell against the coffin.

The sudden jolt threw Snow White against the glass, dislodged the poisoned apple which had been trapped in her throat. As the Prince came closer, Snow White opened her eyes, gasping for air.

The Prince lifted the lid. Snow White was alive again!

"Good heavens, where am I and who are you?" she asked.

The Prince, amazed by the sight before his eyes, replied:

"You, you are on top of the mountain near the house of the seven dwarfs. We all thought you were dead!"

He told her everything that had happened before saying:

"Come with me; we must seek revenge, this evil Queen must be stopped before she hurts you or anyone else ever again!"

Snow White thought for a second, looked at the Prince and said:

"You know, I feel sorry for the Queen and her jealousy filled heart. I think having to live with such jealousy and unhappiness is the worst punishment I could ever imagine.

Let her be unhappy for the rest of her life; I don't want to waste my time thinking about her, ever again!"

The young Prince, perplexed, responded:

"How wise you are, Snow White. I've never thought about that before, but you are right! I don't care about the evil Queen, let her be jealous and miserable until the end of her days."

Snow White smiled and answered: *"Come quick, let's jump on your horse and ride to the house. I want to see the dwarfs; I miss them! They will be so happy to see that I am not dead!"*

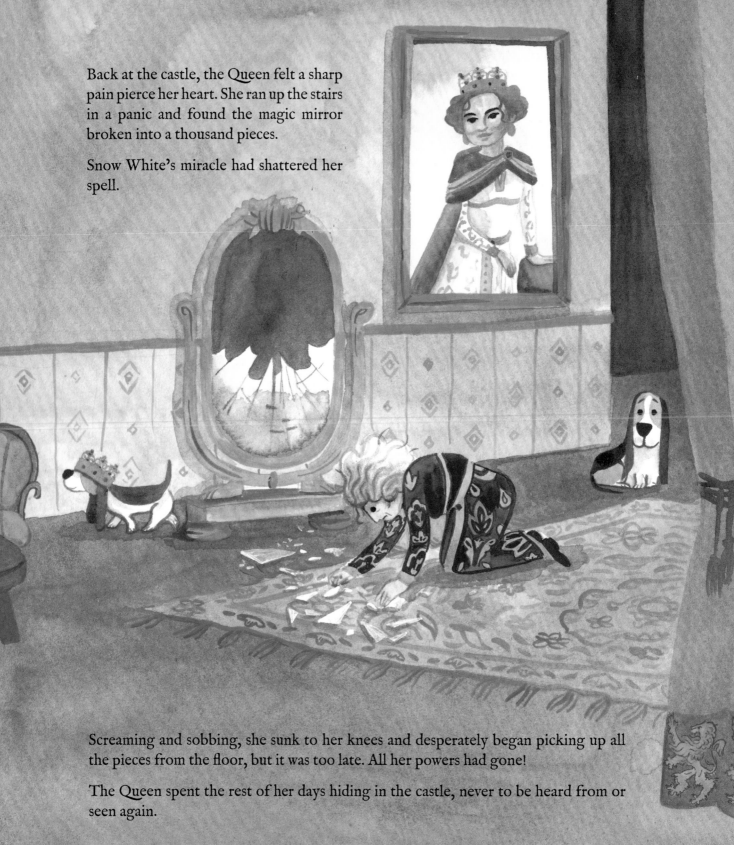

Back at the castle, the Queen felt a sharp pain pierce her heart. She ran up the stairs in a panic and found the magic mirror broken into a thousand pieces.

Snow White's miracle had shattered her spell.

Screaming and sobbing, she sunk to her knees and desperately began picking up all the pieces from the floor, but it was too late. All her powers had gone!

The Queen spent the rest of her days hiding in the castle, never to be heard from or seen again.

Snow White and the Prince arrived back at the house where the dwarfs were overcome with joy. They decided to skip work that day and instead invited all the animals from the forest to their home.

Together they enjoyed a delicious feast together and celebrated this wonderful day by singing and dancing.

The Prince and the Princess talked all day and all night and became close friends.

At the end of the night, after all the animals and the dwarfs had fallen asleep Snow White, who was tidying up with the Prince, turned to him and said:

"You know, this experience has taught me so much. Life is so short and precious. I think I will leave tomorrow to discover the seven corners of the world that the dwarfs have been telling me so much about.

I have been planning it for such a long time; I do not want to delay it anymore!

Why don't you join me, and we can discover this beautiful world together? I could use a friend.

It's hard being brave by yourself all the time." she said with a smile.

The Prince remained silent for a moment, then jumped up and said:

"What a wonderful, wonderful idea! Of course, I will join you.

Tomorrow, we will discover the world together!"

The next morning, at breakfast, Snow White told the seven of their plans. The dwarfs were sad to lose the Princess again, but they understood.

Snow White wiped a tear from her cheek, hugged and kissed each of them; promising to return and tell them all about her adventures.

Snow White and the Prince packed some food and drink and jumped on their horses. With faces full of excitement and joy, they waved to the dwarfs as they rode off into the distance, knowing that their adventures together were just getting started.

And that, dear children, is the *real* story of
Snow White and the Seven Dwarfs.

THE END

Creating this book has been a magical journey. A journey made possible by
a group of glorious people and good friends from around the world.

You helped us slay dragons and joined us on our personal fairy tale. For all
your encouragement inspiration and excitement, we can only say:

Thank You!

Snow White 1 yo   Snow White 3 yo   Snow White 7 yo   Snow White 17 yo   Thiago   Shakti   Sabrina   Li   Leyla   Egbo   Akashi

Snow White is a 19th century German fairy tale.

Originally written in 1812, Snow White has been retold numerous times.

We believe in the magic of fairy tales and have retold this classic to create an empowering narrative for children far and wide.

ISBN: 978-1-5272-5106-9 (Hardcover)

Illustrations by Claudia Piras
Written by Stephan Kalinski & Iain Botterill
Typesetting and Cover design by Sabrina Russo
Layout Design by Stephan Kalinski, Claudia Piras & Sabrina Russo

Printed in Germany by Spree Druck Berlin

First printing: November 2019.

Instinctively Limited

www.fairytales-retold.com

Fairy Tales Retold was created to inspire imaginations and to share
beautiful stories which can be both read and heard.

The audio version of Snow White and the Seven Dwarfs can be
found for all to enjoy at **fairytales-retold.com**

We hope you find it magical to listen to!